Don't Judge a Bird by its Feathers

Written and Illustrated by
Tori Nighthawk

anne stone
PUBLISHING

anne stone PUBLISHING • 468 N. Camden Drive, 2nd Floor • Beverly Hills, CA 90210 • annestonepublishing.com

Publisher's Cataloging-In-Publication Data

Nighthawk, Tori.

Don't judge a bird by its feathers / written & illustrated by Tori Nighthawk. -- 1st ed. -- Beverly Hills, CA :
Anne Stone Pub., c2013.

p. : ill. ; cm.

ISBN: 978-0-9858811-9-1 (hardcover) ; 978-0-9858811-3-9 (ebk.)

Audience: 4+.

SUMMARY: 13-year-old Tori Nighthawk tells the story of two birds of paradise who find that perseverance and creativity can produce big rewards, and that surface appearances are far less important than character, while interweaving facts about the animals of the New Guinea rain forest. --Publisher.

1. Rain forest animals--New Guinea--Juvenile fiction. 2. Persistence--Juvenile fiction. 3. Creative thinking--Juvenile fiction. 4. Physical-appearance-based bias--Juvenile fiction. 5. Character--Juvenile fiction. 6. Bullying--Juvenile fiction. 7. Interpersonal relations--Juvenile fiction. 8. Values--Juvenile fiction. 9. [Rain forest animals--New Guinea--Fiction. 10. Persistance--Fiction. 11. Creative thinking--Fiction. 12. Character--Fiction. 13. Bullying--Fiction. 14. Interpersonal relations--Fiction. 15. Values--Fiction.] I. Title.

PZ7.N5842 D66 2013   2012954786
[Fic]--dc23   1302

All original artwork: Tori Nighthawk

Book design: Isaac Hernández
Author photographs: Starla Fortunato
Flora and fauna photographs: Alaska Stock LLC/National Geographic Stock, Brian J. Skerry/National Geographic Stock, Doug Janson, Laurie Epstein/National Geographic Stock, Mikael Bauer, Nick Baker/EcologyAsia, Paul Sutherland/National Geographic Stock, Peter Woodard, Shaun Tierney/SeaFocus, Tim Laman

First Edition 10 9 8 7 6 5 4 3 2 1
First printing May 2013
Printed in the United States of America by Worzalla, Stevens Point, WI

FSC
www.fsc.org

MIX
Paper from
responsible sources
FSC® C002589

Dedicated to my mom.

Thank you for reading to me when I was little.

Love, Tori

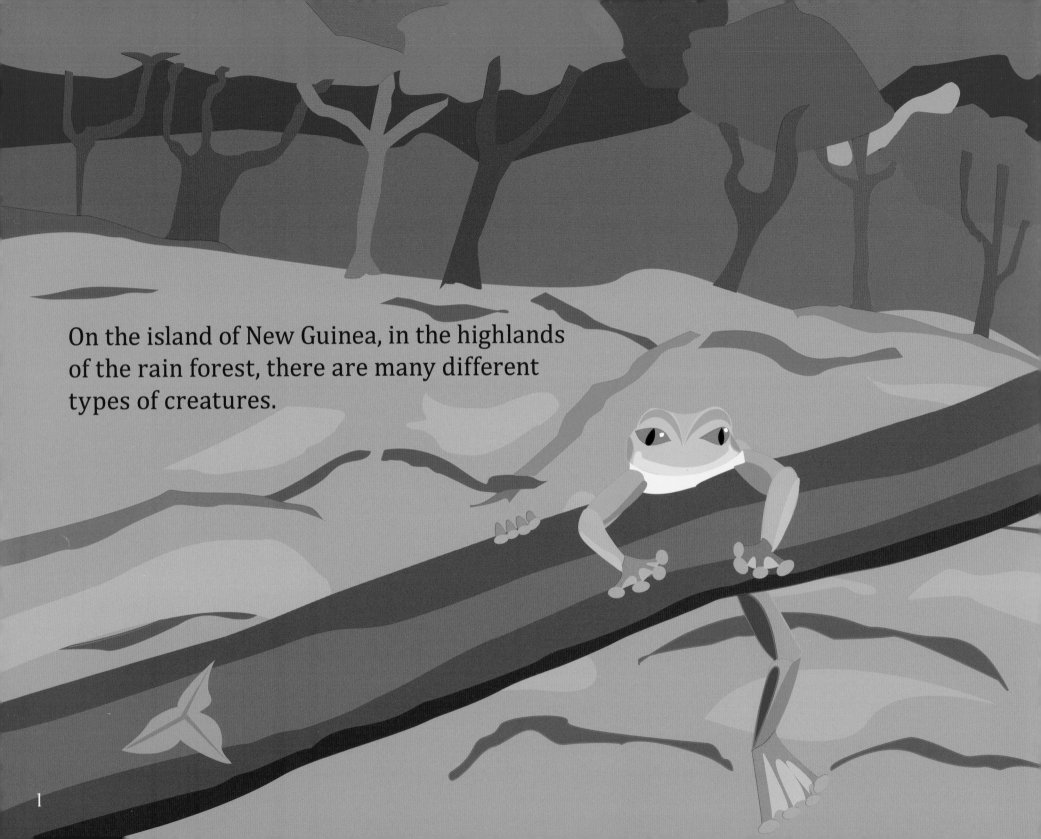

On the island of New Guinea, in the highlands of the rain forest, there are many different types of creatures.

Some are ordinary, like the frogs and dragonflies.

3

Others are unique, like the platypus and the echidna.

While all the animals are special, the most beautiful are the birds of paradise.

To attract the girl's attention,
they dance all day and show off
their magnificent plumage.

6

The prettiest of all the birds of paradise lives in the Highlands. Her parents named her Luminous because her feathers shine like sunlight.

Phoenix also lives high in the mountains.
He is very smart and quite clever.
Unfortunately, for a bird of paradise,
his feathers are anything but colorful.

Every time he tried to dance
like the other male birds,
they laughed and teased him.

"Cahcaa-aah! Cahcaa-aah! Cahcaa-aah!" they
twittered. "How dull and plain you are! You'll
never win the girl's attention dancing like that!"

Phoenix felt so sad, he flew away.

Down,
  down,
    down the mountain he went.

When he reached a sandy beach, he decided to rest on a large leathery rock covered with seven ridges.

While resting on the rock, he watched the seabirds glide and dive into the ocean to catch fish.

He listened to the thunderous sound of the waves crashing on the white sandy beach, and breathed in the crisp, salty air.

Suddenly, the rock began to move!
A large head with two dark eyes met
Phoenix's.

"Hello, little bird," the rock said.

Phoenix shuddered. "Well, hello," he replied in a shaky voice. "You seem to know who I am, but who are you?"

"I am Great Turtle, a leatherback," he answered proudly. "Why have you flown down from the Highlands?"

Phoenix lowered his head. "I had to fly away. The other birds tease me because I am so plain and can't dance as well as they can. They are right, I'm not a good dancer. I feel so sad. I'll never be able to win Luminous' heart."

"Who is Luminous?" Great Turtle asked.

"Luminous," Phoenix answered, "is the most beautiful bird of paradise in all the Highlands. I have loved her since we were chicks."

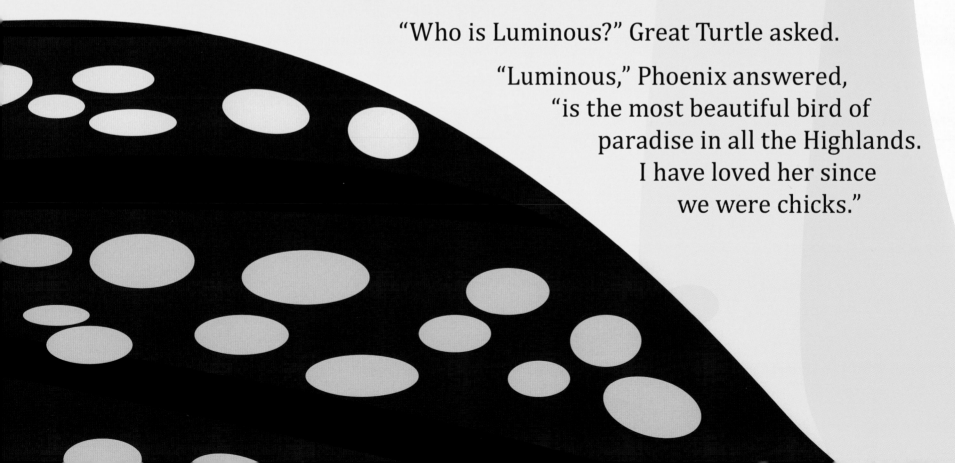

16

"There are many ways to attract a girl,"
Great Turtle shared. "For instance,
our rusa deer show bravery by
fighting for their females.

The rainforest's bowerbirds make a home to impress their future mates.

Humans make a gift of gold-rimmed clam shells."

"Birds of paradise don't do any of those things.
Instead, they dance to impress girls. But when
I try to dance, they laugh and tease me."

Great Turtle thought for a minute.
"Maybe you could practice
dancing in private?"

Phoenix raised a feather.
"That might work!"

up the mountain to the Highlands.

up,

So Phoenix flew up,

Luminous' beautiful colors made her easy to find. But Phoenix's heart sank when he saw her. She was on the forest floor surrounded by dancing males!

The king bird of paradise spun his tail around his head, then swung back and forth on a branch.

The six-plumed bird of paradise puffed up his feathers and shook his head.

The superb bird of paradise
raised his wings, puffed out
his chest, and hop-hop-hopped.

Still, Phoenix was determined to win Luminous' heart. He flew to a quiet cove to practice.

First he puffed his chest, next he shook his head, then he raised his wings and hop-hop-hopped.

Finally, he took a deep breath, then spun his tail around and swung back and forth on a nearby branch.

"That is much better," Phoenix told himself... until giggles from a nearby kwila tree told him otherwise. When he turned around and looked up, he saw Luminous and her friends, laughing.

"Cahcaa-aah! Cahcaa-aah! Cahcaa-aah!" they twittered. Phoenix was mortified.

Again, he flew down,
down,
down the mountain to talk with Great Turtle.

"Luminous laughed at me!"
Phoenix cried.

Then he shared his sad, sad tale.

"There, there, little bird," Great
Turtle said, trying to comfort him.

"I do believe I have the solution to
your problem. Look in the sand.
Tell me, what do you see?"

"I see a beautiful shell,"
Phoenix replied.

"And what's inside that shell?"

"A crab," Phoenix answered.

"See!" Great Turtle said. "The plain hermit crab is dressed up in a beautiful shell that had been tossed aside by another sea animal!"

So, once again, Phoenix flew up, up, up the mountain. He had a clever idea! He scoured the rainforest looking for beautiful discarded feathers. He looked under ferns, in the creeper vines, and all around the forest floor. But all he could find were the feathers of the harpy eagle.

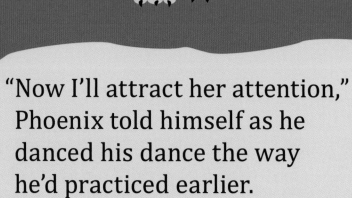

Determined, he wove those feathers
into his own, then pranced about
like a handsome bird of paradise.

"Now I'll attract her attention,"
Phoenix told himself as he
danced his dance the way
he'd practiced earlier.

But then, giggles from a nearby
kwila tree told him otherwise.

When he turned around, there sat Luminous
and her friends, laughing even louder this time.

"Cahcaa-aah! Cahcaa-aah! Cahcaa-aah!" they twittered.

Again, Phoenix flew down, down, down the mountain, only this time he flew faster than he'd ever flown before.

Great Turtle listened to
Phoenix's sad, sad tale.

"I see you're dressed in the feathers
of another," Great Turtle said.

39

"That reminds me of one of the most intelligent creatures in the ocean: the great mimic octopus."

"Whenever a fish wants to eat him, he makes himself look like a sea krait sea snake, to scare the fish away."

"If sea snakes eat the fish, what eats the sea snake?" Phoenix asked.

Great Turtle didn't know for sure. But he did know that eagles prey on tree snakes.

"Eagles eat birds of paradise too!" Phoenix said.

Phoenix felt better after talking to Great Turtle. He loved learning new things.

Phoenix decided to bring a gift to impress Luminous. He gathered up some gold-rimmed clam shells from the salty seashore, then up, up, up the mountain he flew.

As he flew, he enjoyed the fresh lemon scent of the dough wood tree's fragrant leaves and looked at their beautiful pink flowers.

He was thinking that this was his very favorite smell when a shrill "Creeeeeee! Creeeeeeee! Creeeeeee!" interrupted his thoughts.

A bird of paradise was in trouble!

Phoenix followed the sounds of the terrified bird, and flew into the canopy of dough woods.

45

There, pressed against the tree's thick brown trunk, staring straight into the mouth of a green tree python, was his beautiful Luminous!

Phoenix instantly swooped in to save her, accidently dropping his shiny, gold-rimmed clam shells on the python's head.

The python turned to face Phoenix!

Instinctively, Phoenix puffed himself up, spreading his wings, feather after feather, including those he'd borrowed from the forest floor.

Terrified, the bright green snake backed away and slithered down the tree. He had mistaken Phoenix for his enemy, the harpy eagle!

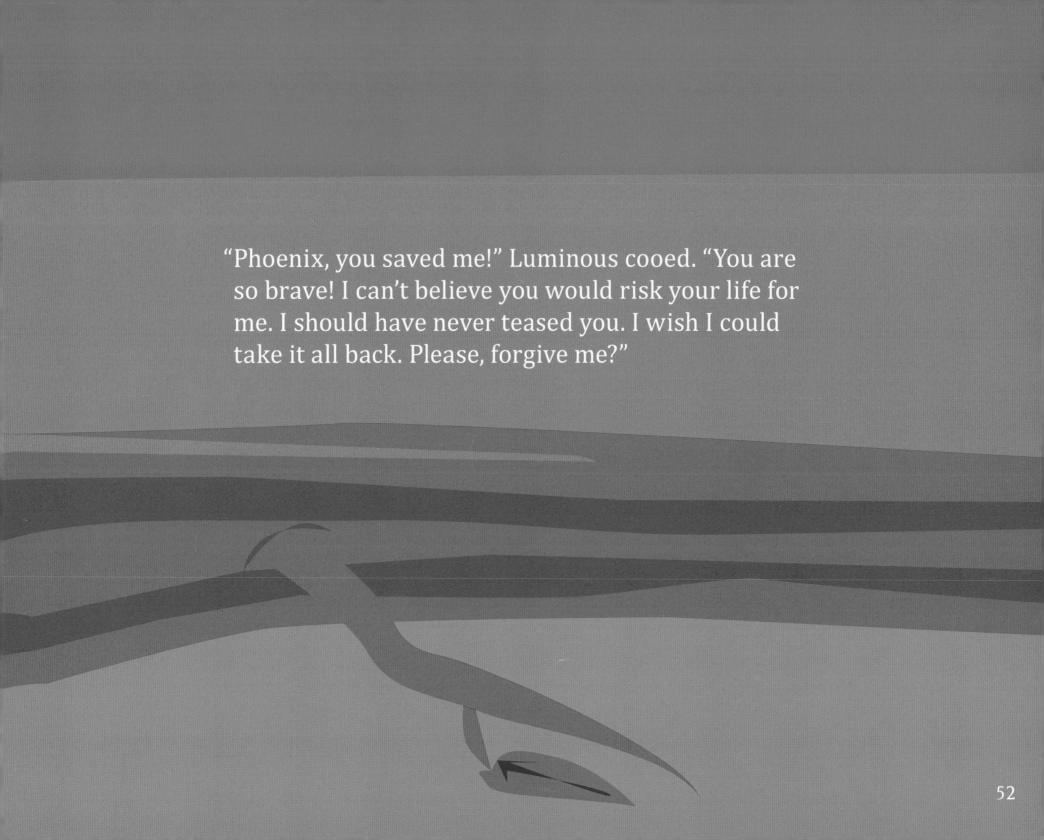

"Phoenix, you saved me!" Luminous cooed. "You are so brave! I can't believe you would risk your life for me. I should have never teased you. I wish I could take it all back. Please, forgive me?"

As time passed,
Luminous fell in love with Phoenix.
She loved his quick wit, his strong spirit,
and his brave heart.

Luminous loved Phoenix for
who he is on the inside.

Birds of Paradise

Blue Bird of Paradise

The Blue Bird of Paradise lives in the mountain forests of central and southeastern New Guinea. It's a medium-sized bird of paradise measuring up to 11.8in (30cm) in length, excluding the long ribbon-like tail feathers with blue ends on the male. Both male and female have a blue-black body with blue wings and a pale beak. They have a broken white eye-ring and grey legs and feet. The female is reddish-brown underneath. The male is adorned with violet blue and cinnamon flank plumes, and cinnamon tail plumes. He displays these to a female by hanging upside down and flaring them out in a big fan. He makes a buzzing sound at her and waves the fan of plumes back and forth. There is a red-rimmed black oval disk on his chest he repeatedly flares during the courting display. The males are solitary performers, calling to females from a high perch on the ridgeline at least 219 yards (200m) away from other males. When a female arrives, the display takes place on a low branch with the wings remaining closed. The females build and perform all the nesting duties. They eat fruit and insects. (Pg. 5)

Curl-crested Manucode

The male Curl-crested Manucode, like other manucodes but unlike other birds of paradise, is monogamous, and stays with one female for his whole adult life. At 17in (43cm) long, he's much heavier than other birds of paradise. The blue-black bird's iridescent purples and greens shine in the dark. It has twisted central tail feathers. The female looks similar to the male but is slightly smaller. These birds forage for food in groups, and sometimes with the Goldie's Bird of Paradise. They eat fruit. The female lays two eggs in a nest built of twigs and leaves high up in a tree fork. (Pg. 8)

Goldie's Bird of Paradise

Goldie's Bird of Paradise lives in the hilly rainforest of two small islands of New Guinea. They are about 13in (33cm) long. The female has olive-brown top feathers, cinnamon brown feathers underneath, a yellow crown and nape and dark feathers under the chin. The male has yellow on the head and back, with a green chin and a lavender gray chest. In addition to two long tail wires, he has long crimson side feathers in two layers, which he puffs up and out during courting of multiple females. He shares his display area of about four trees with other males. They all pluck leaves during courting, so this area has less leaves. The female raises her chick alone. Their main diet is fruit, but unlike other birds of paradise, they also search in the undergrowth for insects. (Pg. 7)

Find the flora and fauna in this glossary throughout the book. Use the page numbers on each of the paragraphs to help you on your book safari.

King Bird of Paradise

The King Bird of Paradise is common in New Guinea and the surrounding islands. It is the smallest of the birds of paradise, being only 6in (16cm) long. The male is red on top, with a white belly and bright green feathers just below the head, and two long tail wires with emerald green disks at the end. Both male and female have bright blue feet and legs. The female is brown with a little cinnamon on the sides, and barring on her undersides. The male courting ritual includes pulling the tail wires up over the head, puffing out his white chest like a balloon, and swinging the tail. He also hangs upside down and swings like a pendulum. The female builds a nest in cavities and forks of lower trees, and raises her chicks alone. Their diet consists of fruit and insects. (Pg. 23)

© Tim Laman/TimLaman.com

Lesser Bird of Paradise

© Doug Janson/www.pbase.com/dougi

The Lesser Bird of Paradise lives in lowland rainforests and swamp forests. It is 12.5in (32cm) long, and eats fruit, insects, and sometimes even snails. The male is a maroon-brown bird with a yellow crown, yellow eyes and an emerald green throat. It has a pair of long tail wires, and ornamental flank plumes. These plumes, bright yellow fading to white at the ends, are displayed while courting females. The display is performed in a group setting called a lek. The female is also maroon-brown, but it has a dark brown head and is white on the underside. The female builds a bulky nest high up in a tree with twigs and dead leaves. She lines it with black fibers, and lays one to two pinkish eggs with dark markings. (Pg. 5)

© Tim Laman/TimLaman.com

Superb Bird of Paradise

The Superb Bird of Paradise lives in the mountainous rainforest on two small islands of New Guinea. The 10in (25cm) female is brown, lighter beneath. The male clears an area of the forest for his stage, and puffs out his iridescent blue chest feathers and black wings to make quite an unusual and beautiful appearance. He then dances and hops around until the female is pleased with him. The female lays her egg in a twig nest in a tree. After 18 to 20 days, a bald chick hatches and is cared for by the mother until it grows feathers and can fly. These birds eat mostly fruit, but some seeds, insects, frogs and lizards. (Pg. 24)

© Tim Laman/TimLaman.com

Vogelkop Bowerbird

The medium-size Vogelkop Bowerbird lives in the mountains of the Vogelkop Peninsula in Western New Guinea. The male is 10in (25cm) long and the female slightly smaller. They are both olive brown and a little paler on the underside. This bird is less ornamental than most other bowerbirds, but the male builds one of the largest and most elaborate bower nests, a cone-shaped hut 39in (100cm) high and 62in (160cm) in diameter. He decorates the "front yard" with moss and colorful fruits and flowers, taking up to 9 months each year on his creation. The female carefully inspects his work before deciding whether she likes it. If she does, she goes inside the nest, thus accepting the male. Curiously, neither he nor his bower nest play a part in the nesting and raising of the young. The female builds a nest of soft plant materials, lays one to two eggs, and attends to all the nesting duties. Bowerbirds eat mostly fruit and flowers, but may also feed on insects, leaves and nectar. (Pg. 18)

© Tim Laman/TimLaman.com

Western Parotia

The Western Parotia is a six-plumed bird of paradise, found only in the Vogelkop forest and the Wandammen Peninsula in Western New Guinea. The male is 13in (33cm) long, and the female is 11.8in (30cm) long. The female is chestnut brown with a pale barred underside. The male is jet black with a golden/green breast shield, a silver triangle on his crown, and three head wires behind each eye. He has elongated black plumes at the side of his breast that he flares out during his courting display, when he dances with an amazing ballerina style, and waves his body back and forth causing the breast shield to alternate colors. The female attends to all the nesting duties alone. Their main diet consists of fruit. (Pg. 6, 23)

© Doug Janson/www.pbase.com/dougj

Wilson's Bird of Paradise

Wilson's Bird of Paradise, a small bird only 8in (21cm) long including its curled silvery purple tail wires, is found in the hills and lowland rainforests of two little islands of New Guinea. The male clears an area of leaves so the sun can show off his colors as he calls to females, and then displays for them. The male is black, with a red back and a patch of green on the breast. He also has a yellow mantle on his neck, a green breast and a yellowish green mouth. The female is brown with barring on its lighter underside. Both male and female have a bald turquoise blue head with black markings. The display involves posturing with the shield up around the neck and the curly tail wires pulled up. The females build and attend to nesting by themselves. Their diet consists of fruit and small insects. (Pg. 5)

Additional Fauna and Flora of New Guinea

Dough Wood Tree

The Dough Wood is a rainforest tree which grows to 82ft (25m) tall and has a 2ft (60cm) trunk diameter. The trunk has a doughy look, and a soft, almost-white layer of cork-like, dead bark. The green leaflets come in threes and can be 6–13in (15–33cm) long. It has a pleasant citrus-like scent, and its pretty pink flowers attract butterflies. (Pg. 45)

© Peter Woodard

Dragonfly

There are over 400 kinds of dragonflies in New Guinea. Most of them are very beautiful and colorful. Their larvae live in water and can be used to see if the water is pure, because very few will tolerate salty water. The larvae prey on small animals, even tadpoles and tiny or baby fish. Adult dragonflies catch insects with their feet to eat. The adults live up to a year. (Pg. 2)

© Tim Laman/TimLaman.com

© Tim Laman/TimLaman.com

Echidna

The Echidna is one of only two egg-laying mammals in the world. They have spines similar to a hedgehog. New Guinea echidna have a long curved snout with electro-sensors to help locate food, and a long sticky tongue with spines on the end to help hold onto the earthworms and larvae they love to eat. The mother echidna lays just one soft leathery egg directly into her pouch. The babies are called puggles. The echidna grow to be up to 16in (40cm) long and weigh as much as 35lbs (16.5kg), but are more likely to be 15–20lbs (6.8–9kg). They fear their predator, the harpy eagle. (Pg. 4)

© Nick Baker/EcologyAsia.com

Green Tree Python

The Green Tree Python lives in the trees of New Guinea and Australia. The adults are 3–4.5ft (90–120cm) in length, and have a bright green back with a lighter belly and back markings. Some are bluish in color, and many have blue, yellow, or brown markings. The young are mostly yellow, but may be red, orange, or brown, and become green at 6–8 months. They eat small animals, which they catch by hanging onto a branch with their tails, before striking and constricting. (Pg. 46)

© Brian J. Skerry/Nat'l Geographic Stock

Giant Leatherback Sea Turtle

The giant Leatherback Sea Turtle is not only bigger than other sea turtles, but has other differences as well. Their shells are leathery with seven ridges, their front flippers are longer, and they swim faster and dive deeper. Their main diet is jellyfish. They are dark gray to black, with white spots on the top. The underside is lighter. Adults average 6–7.2ft (1.8–2.2m) weighing 550–1500lbs (250–700kg). They travel great distances in the world's oceans. The female lays her eggs on the sand. Hatchlings must make it to the open sea to survive, and are vulnerable to predators until they are larger. The Leatherback Turtle is an endangered species. If the turtle makes it to adulthood it may live 30 to 50 years. (Pg. 13)

© Mikael Bauer

Harpy Eagle

The New Guinea Harpy Eagle is a large bird of prey, who lives in the rainforest, avoiding open areas. They grow to be up to 35in (90cm) long, with a wingspan of 62in (157cm), and a short full crest. They hunt for small animals and snakes at night, dropping from a perch, running along on the ground and pouncing on their prey, or using their claws to reach into tree cavities to pull their prey out. A pair of harpy eagles raises one chick at a time, in a huge nest, high up in the trees. (Pg. 31)

© Shaun Tierney/SeaFocus.com

Mimic Octopus

The Mimic Octopus has pigment sacs on its skin, which it can make bigger or smaller to change patterns and colors. Most animals that can change their colors use this skill to help them hide from predators and prey by blending in. The Mimic Octopus, however, changes to look like different venomous animals, and even copies their movements, scaring off predators who would normally eat it. Mimics have been seen imitating sea snakes, lionfish, stingrays, flatfish, jellyfish and more. They are so intelligent they even know which animal will frighten each predator. When at rest, the Mimic Octopus is a light brown with white stripes or spots. It grows up to 2ft (60cm) long. The eight tentacles are about 10in (25cm) long, and thin like a pencil. They like to live in depths as far down as 49ft (15m) on muddy and sandy ocean bottoms in Indonesia and Malaysia. (Pg. 39)

Platypus

The Platypus is a semi-aquatic mammal that digs burrows in riverbanks and fresh water lakes. During the day it sleeps in the burrow, or basks in the sun and grooms its fur. After dusk and before dawn it spends several hours diving down into the water to dig up insect larvae, shrimp and worms to eat. The platypus closes its eyes and ears while under water, but its duck-like bill has electroreceptors that can sense even tiny movements. The webbed, clawed feet, similar to an otter's, help it swim. At 2–5lbs (1–2.4kg), the platypus may look cuddly, but beware; the male has a hollow spur on its hind ankles which can inject strong venom into an enemy. After mating during the summer, the female lays two leathery eggs, which she holds against her warm tummy with her beaver-like tail to incubate for a couple of weeks. When the eggs hatch, the baby platypus has no hair, and the young are nursed through milk patches in the mother's fur for four months. (Pg. 3)

© Jason Edwards/National Geographic Stock

© Alaska Stock LLC/National Geographic Stock

Razor Clam

The Razor Clam likes to bury into the sand, attaching its pointed end to the rock. The fan shape opening is very sharp and can cut open your foot if accidently stepped on. At high tide they open their shell to let a current of water through. They filter the water, looking for plankton or other small animals in the water. These clams are harvested as a popular food. (Pg. 18)

© Lori Epstein/National Geographic Stock

Rusa Deer

Rusa Deer live in New Guinea and eat a wide variety of plants. They have even been seen swimming in the ocean and eating seaweed. They are social, and live in herds. Rusa deer are about 40in (102cm) tall at the shoulder and 65in (165cm) long. The tail is 7–8 in (20cm) long. Only the male deer have antlers. Deer are mammals, and the calves drink their mother's milk. (Pg. 17)

Sea Krait

The Banded Sea Krait is highly venomous, but not aggressive to human divers. They can hold their breath for up to three hours. The males are about 34 in (86cm) long, and the much larger females are about 55 in (140cm). Sea kraits hunt for fish such as surgeonfish and damselfish. These fish are faster than them, so the snakes work together to catch them among the coral and rocks. Their dangerous venom paralizes the fish so they can't swim away. (Pg. 41)

© Shaun Tierney/SeaFocus.com

Sooty Tern

Tern seabirds spend most of their time looking for small fish at sea, and nest in colonies on the shore. There are 16 kinds of terns on the island of New Guinea. The Sooty Tern looks dark on the ground, but white during flight because his undersides are mostly white. A colony can be so loud that it is nicknamed the "Wideawake," as it won't let you sleep. The Sooty Tern nests on rocky or coral islands. The female will lay one to three eggs in a depression or hole. Their lifespan is 32 years. These terns may stay out to sea three to ten years at a time, either flying or floating. They are 13–14in (33–36cm) long, and have a wingspan of 34–37in (82–94cm). (Pg. 14)

© Tim Laman/TimLaman.com

© Shaun Tierney/SeaFocus.com

© Paul Sutherland/National Geographic Stock

White-Spotted Hermit Crab

The White-Spotted Hermit Crab, the largest hermit crab in the area, grows to 4in (10cm). Some species prefer to live in the ocean while others live on land. They eat most anything they can find, including plants and dead animals. They pick food and water droplets up with their claws and reach it to their mouth. Their bodies are soft and need to be in a shell for protection. They do not grow their own shells, but move into the empty shells of other species. They change shells when they outgrow them, or when they find another they like better. (Pg. 30)

White-Lipped Tree Frog

The White-Lipped Tree Frog, the world's largest tree frog, grows to 4–5.5in (10–14cm) long, and is sometimes called the Giant Tree Frog. It is usually a bright green, but can change to a rusty brown color depending on temperature or stress. Males call to females each spring to mate. They normally have a barking call, but when afraid they make a cat-like "mew" sound. The tadpoles eat aquatic plants for a month or two before evolving into frogs and climbing out of the water and onto trees where they feed on insects. (Pg. 1)

60

Starla Fortunato/StarlaFortunato.com

Tori Nighthawk is a keen observer of life and a natural storyteller. At the young age of 13, she crafts her observations into fascinating metaphors that impart insight as well as educate. Her writing touches the hearts and minds of readers of all ages in a most unique way.

In addition to writing, Tori is a gifted artist who uses vibrant colors to magically capture the essence of her subjects.

When Tori isn't traveling the world, she lives in Southern California with her parents, her younger brother, and a variety of family pets.

www.ToriNighthawk.com